I WON'T GIVE UP

WRITTEN BY
DANIEL KENNEY
ILLUSTRATED BY
SUMIT ROY

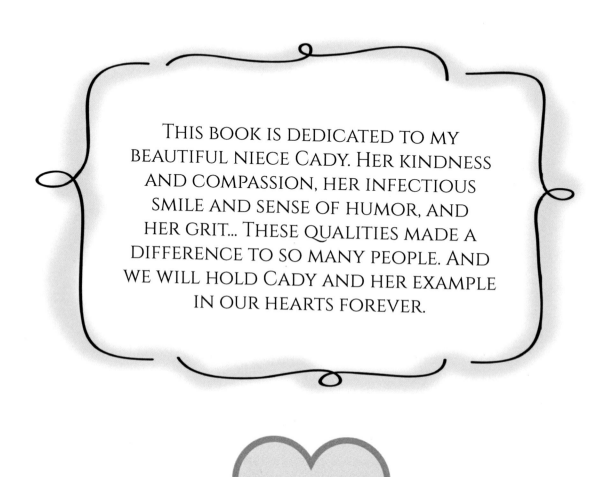

THIS BOOK IS DEDICATED TO MY BEAUTIFUL NIECE CADY. HER KINDNESS AND COMPASSION, HER INFECTIOUS SMILE AND SENSE OF HUMOR, AND HER GRIT... THESE QUALITIES MADE A DIFFERENCE TO SO MANY PEOPLE. AND WE WILL HOLD CADY AND HER EXAMPLE IN OUR HEARTS FOREVER.

HI, MY NAME IS CADY.

Sometimes, I feel embarrassed when I can't tie my shoes.

I HAVE TO ASK MY GRANDMA FOR HELP.

OR WEAR THE LITTLE KID SHOES WITH THE BRIGHT VELCRO STRAPS.

LEARNING TO TIE SHOES IS HARD.

IT CAN BE FRUSTRATING.

BUT I'LL KEEP TRYING.

AND I WONT GIVE UP...

UNTIL I REACH MY GOAL!

SOMETIMES, I FEEL SAD WHEN I CAN'T RIDE MY BIKE.

IT FEELS LIKE EVERYONE CAN RIDE EXCEPT ME.

AND THE ONLY BIKE I USE HAS ENORMOUS TRAINING WHEELS.

LEARNING TO RIDE A BIKE IS HARD.

IT CAN BE SCARY.

BUT I'LL KEEP TRYING.

AND I WONT GIVE UP...

UNTIL I REACH MY GOAL!

SOMETIMES, I FEEL DUMB WHEN I CAN'T DO MATH.

I'M WORRIED MY BRAIN ISN'T BUILT LIKE THE OTHER KIDS.

AND THAT I'LL NEVER BE ABLE TO FIGURE IT OUT.

LEARNING TO DO MATH IS HARD.

IT CAN BE FRUSTRATING.

BUT I'LL KEEP TRYING.

AND I WONT GIVE UP...

UNTIL I REACH MY GOAL!

SOMETIMES, I FEEL FRUSTRATED WHEN I TRY TO PLAY THE PIANO.

IT FEELS LIKE I'VE GOT NOTHING BUT THUMBS.

AND THE NOISES I MAKE SCARE EVERYONE.

LEARNING THE PIANO IS HARD.

IT CAN BE FRUSTRATING.

BUT I'LL KEEP TRYING

AND
I
WONT
GIVE
UP...

UNTIL I REACH MY GOAL!

BUT OF ALL THE THINGS THAT ARE HARD FOR ME,
HITTING A BALL IS THE WORST.

THE OTHER TEAM IS SCARED OF ME BECAUSE
MY BAT GOES FARTHER THAN THE BALL.

THE ONLY WAY I'D BE ABLE TO HIT THE BALL IS
WITH THE BIGGEST BAT IN THE WORLD.

HITTING A BALL IS HARD.

IT CAN BE FRUSTRATING. SO FRUSTRATING.

BUT I'LL KEEP TRYING

AND I WONT GIVE UP!

Until I finally reach my goal!

Sometimes, things in life can be difficult.

They can be frustrating!

But remember, you can do it.

Don't give up until you reach your goal.

Instructions For Parents and Trusted Adults:

Persisting when things are tough is an essential habit for a life of happiness and success. But there are some things to consider.

First, nobody can win everything, no matter how hard you try. But a well-lived life is all about the "trying". And building an "I Won't Give Up" attitude should always be encouraged even if, sometimes, the goal is not actually met.

Second, there does come a time in life when one does actually need to quit something. Some situations are so unhealthy that they make a person miserable at a deep level, and no amount of "not quitting" is going to do anything more for that person.

What are children to do in these situations?

Children should always feel comfortable going to their parents, guardians, and mentors when activities are making them unhappy.

It is a trusted adult's job to help the child figure out whether this occasion calls for persistence… or the wisdom to humbly quit and move on to a healthier activity.

Finally, consider spending some time right now talking with your children about something in their lives that is challenging and frustrating. Can you help them think of ways they can try harder? Can you help them think of ways they can try a different strategy? Encourage them to "not give up" in this particular activity. Tell them you will check back in with them in one week to see how they are doing with their challenge. And speaking of challenges, maybe there is something you want to work on for yourself. Consider sharing your challenge with your children and they can ask you about it in one week to see how you are doing as well.

Cover: Alchemy Book Covers
Illustrations: Sumit Roy
Interior formatting: Polgarus Studio

Made in the USA
Lexington, KY
21 September 2018